'Little Spirit was ama
from start to finish kep
very last paragraph had a small, intriguing twist.'
Holly, age 10

'I really enjoyed this book and think that it is
brilliant. I also enjoyed the suspense and I would
recommend this book for lots of other children.'
Bethany, age 8

'It was brilliant! It was really well written and I loved Little Spirit. It was really gripping and I couldn't wait to find out what happened at the end.'
Sebastian, age 10

'I loved Little Spirit! I would recommend it to ages 8 to 12 as it's not too complicated or too babyish. Overall I would go give it a…10/10!'
Eliza, age 9

'A dramatic and epic adventure!'
Ellie, age 9

'When I finished reading the book I wanted to know more about how Little Spirit lost his family. I would like you to make a sequel to this book and I would love to read it, as well as any other book you write.'
Ethan, age 9

LITTLE SPIRIT

BY

A J FREER

First published in 2018

by A J Freer

First Amazon Edition

Copyright © A J Freer 2018

ISBN: 978-1-790258-16-1

Editorial support & proofreading, Meghan Thompson

Editorial support, Jonathan Eyers

Cover design by A J Freer

For Mark, Rocco and Cristabel, my little family.

And for all the lost sons and daughters, while you are far from home, may you live in safety and find peace.

1

AN UNUSUAL FOG

It was an unusual fog that fell that night, it billowed around and came down over town like the flick of a cloth over a table. And lost in the middle of that thick, swirling cloud was a double-decker bus and a boy.

'Wretched fog!' snapped the bus driver, suddenly not able to see the road. He pressed the brake, slowing the bus down to a trundle, and flicked on the fog-lights. Leaning forwards over the steering wheel he squinted through his glasses at the misty fronds twisting and twining in the headlights. 'Don't like the fog,' he grumbled, 'brings out the–'

He stopped.

'Wassat?' He shook his head and blinked. 'Never seen a green one!' he croaked, watching a shadowy lump hurtle towards him.

CRUNCH!

The bus stopped and the driver sat for a moment staring at the blanket of leaves pressed against the window. 'Hedge,' he muttered, smiling faintly with relief. With another shake of his head and a roar of the engine, he reversed back onto the road.

'But I still 'ate the fog. Brings out them ghosts, makes everythin' act...strange, but, no one on board, so NO stoppin'! Won't be letting them ghouls inside,' he announced to the apparently empty vehicle.

Only the bus wasn't empty. In fact, someone was listening. Someone very small. Someone very alone. Someone sat in the corner seat of the very back row, curled up tight like a cat.

His name was Little Spirit.

He was thin and pale like the rain, but with hair as dark as cocoa. He wore a ragged coat and shorts, and carried nothing. Not a thing. Not even a little rucksack, or an apple for emergencies, not even a picture of his family – despite being a very long way from home.

He had hidden on the first bus he'd seen at the huge depot and travelled alone for a whole day and a night. He desperately needed a warm place to rest and although he loved the low rumbling of the engine and the squashy seats, at night-time, when all was quiet, the cold would tiptoe into the bus and turn his bones to ice.

And after nearly being thrown off his seat, he decided it was time to get off.

Little Spirit unfurled and, careful not to

been seen over the seats in front, he stretched a spidery finger up to the stop button.

DING!

The driver wrenched his head around. ''OO'S THERE?' he yelled and careered off the road for the second time that evening.

The brakes shook and then shrieked. And so did the driver. While he battled with the steering wheel, Little Spirit crawled under the seats, hiding behind the panel next to the back doors. A last wail from the engine and the driver finally bumped the bus back onto the road.

'What did I say! Ghosts on me bus!' he muttered, racing to the next stop and screeching to a halt. 'SHOW ye-self!' he bellowed and pressed a button on the dashboard.

Swoosh! The doors flew open.

Little Spirit knew he had only a moment

before the driver would turn and peer behind him, so he jumped out of the bus diving straight into a small fir-tree. He wriggled to a standing position, the sharp wood scratching his skin.

Gently parting the feathery leaves he looked out onto the road, just in time to see his friend, the bus, disappear into the fog. His head dropped and he pressed his eyelids together. Squeezing the branches, he clung tightly to the world fearing if he let go he'd drop right off. *Hang on*, he thought, *hang on and don't cry*. But the harder he squeezed his eyelids the more they overflowed like the slopping water buckets he used to carry up the steep hill to his house.

His lip trembled and his stomach whirled like a hurricane. Perhaps he should have stayed on the bus. Little Spirit looked out into the darkness, and although he knew in the swirl and furl of the misty night he could move safely, he didn't know which way to go. Should he turn left or right? He wished his family was there so they could hold hands and find their way together. He could hardly believe he had lost them, it had been only a few days but it felt like months.

Little Spirit swallowed and brushed the tears from his face. Legs quaking, he wiggled out of the hedge and dashed across the road, hesitating a little, before walking straight into the dark underbelly of a bridge.

There were no lights in the short tunnel and in a few nervous steps he emerged out of the other side. Peering through small breaks in the fog, Little Spirit saw a road leading off to the left and, since it was the only path he could see, he decided to follow it.

One cautious footstep at a time, he weaved

his way up the street, passing a row of narrow houses, one snuggled tightly to another. Dull light pushed out around the curtains of each window and through one set, left half-open, he saw the flicker of a fire. He stopped for a moment, longing to hold his hands up to the warm flames. The soft light drew him nearer until he pressed his nose against the glass and closed his eyes.

Tap! Tap! Tap!

He snapped open his eyes and jumped. On the inside of the window, another nose was pressed against his. Through a jumble of dark curls, two large eyes stared at him. Little Spirit hesitated for a moment before leaping back into the fog.

Worried he might be caught, he ran across the road and crouched behind a brick wall. After a few seconds, he stood up and peeked over the top. Through a gap in the fog, he could see a girl pointing out of the window. She pointed again and started to cry.

Little Spirit ducked down, hoping he hadn't scared her. He looked down at his hands, so pale they could belong to a ghost. Sometimes he almost believed he had become one. Hiding here and there. Keeping out of sight. Slipping left-over food from tables and silently eating sandwich crusts whilst hidden behind large suitcases – the journey from the docks had taught him the craft of invisibility.

He peeked over the top again, but the fog had thickened and he couldn't see across the road. The girl had such kind eyes and he was sorry he had frightened her. But perhaps her mother was comforting her, gently brushing the tears from her cheeks. He didn't like the pain of crying but he longed for the fall of tears that at home would instantly conjure up the loving arms of his mother.

Instead, the cold pinched his bare legs and made him shiver.

Teeth rattling, he stood for a moment wondering what to do next. He couldn't see very far ahead and decided to follow the wall hoping it would lead to a building. At first, the red bricks scraped his hands, but they soon turned into a smooth handrail running upwards above a set of stone steps.

He was about to walk up them when he stopped. Ears pricked, he thought he could hear the tip-tapping of footsteps. Was the girl following him?

Little Spirit didn't want to be followed or

found, all he wanted was a warm place to rest. So he leapt up the steps to the top, stumbling onwards over graves and around trees until–

'Owww!' He quickly clapped his hand over his mouth, sweeping his eyes this way and that. Had anyone heard?

The wind whistled softly and the fog swirled but otherwise the night was silent. Perhaps he hadn't heard footsteps after all.

Peering up, he saw what he had bumped into, another wall but this one was much taller and built of jagged grey stones. Again, he followed the wall, stumbling alongside it, shivering and shaking until finally, he found a door.

A huge wooden door.

Through chattering teeth, he managed a grateful smile; it wasn't any old door, it was a door to be opened – someone had left the key in the lock!

He raised a shaking hand, trying to grip the key. But then he froze. This time he was absolutely certain.

The tap, tap, tap of footsteps hurried towards him.

With one hand steadying the other, Little Spirit grabbed the key and wrenched it as hard as he could. Stuck. He tried again but it wouldn't budge.

The footsteps grew louder.

In desperation, he leant on the door with his shoulder and to his surprise it flew open. He stumbled into the darkness, scrambling under a wooden bench as the door slammed behind him.

Outside, a young man reached the church just after it closed. He stood for a moment, panting, and watched in amazement as the fog lifted as fast as it had arrived; billowing upwards, a cloth snatched away in a flash.

'Astonishing,' he whispered, staring cross-eyed down his nose as the last foggy wisp disintegrated under his nostrils. Still perplexed by the changeable weather, he shrugged his shoulders and dug his hand into his pocket pulling out a crumpled piece of tinfoil. He carefully opened it and scooped up a slippery wedge of butter. Trying not to drop it, he pushed it around the key and into the lock.

'There'll be no more nonsense from you!' he said to the key. He bent his knees and braced himself. 'One. Two. Three!'

Finally, the key turned.

'Gotcha!' said the curate, nodding in triumph and holding up the greasy lump of iron between his finger and thumb.

Inside, Little Spirit listened to the fading footsteps and let out a sigh. He hadn't been discovered. Even better, he was safely locked inside.

He looked quickly around and realised he was in a church. In the faint light streaming down from the glass windows, he crawled out of his hiding place and tiptoed across the stone floor. Something caught his foot and he stumbled. He tried to walk forwards but a strange weight twisted around his ankles and pulled him down.

'Ahhh' he yelled, kicking and flailing on the floor until a gentle flump of material landed on top of him. Lying on his back, he lifted his legs into the air and saw his attacker – a pair of old curtains!

Tears of relief welled in his eyes. He

jumped up, threw one curtain around his shoulders and hugged the other.

Looking down he noticed they had been hiding a pile of cushions. With a smile, he picked them up and, in a dark corner, made himself a nest with cushions. He pulled both curtains tightly around him and closed his eyes.

Safe and warm, Little Spirit fell asleep.

Outside the locked doors, another set of footsteps stopped. A man looked left and right and pulled his hat low over his face. He raised his palm and pushed the door.

2

BANANAS

Click!

Little Spirit woke with a start. His eyes darted round, quickly taking in his vast new home. There were many churches in Guatemala and each year Little Spirit would lie on a plank of wood, suspended above the cobbled streets, and sprinkle coloured sawdust to make the Alfombras, brightly patterned carpets in celebration of Easter.

Clunk!

The wooden door creaked open.

Once again, Little Spirit rolled under the nearest pew, this time whipping the curtains behind him. His stomach lurched with hunger. The first thing he needed to do that day was eat. And when he had food inside him and had found some warm clothes, he would walk back to the bus stop, take the return journey, and find his family.

Footsteps thumped towards him.

'Butter?' muttered a woman's voice.

Peering upwards, Little Spirit watched her pink trainers squidge past him.

Clunk! Another door opened.

'Morning, Luke. You're late today!' the lady called out as the clatter of more footsteps met hers. 'But, look at this, my key is covered in butter! The lock was jammed with it!'

'Ah! That was me, Vicar. I couldn't lock it, butter got it moving!'

'Ingenious! Never've thought of that myself,'

she said, wiping the key on a tissue. 'Dreadful fog last night, but at least it came and went in a flash. I hope it's clear on Remembrance Sunday – we do need to see where to put the wreaths!'

Through a gap in the underside of the bench, Little Spirit could see the two people were dressed mostly in black, with white collars in the necks of their shirts. He barely knew a word of English and tried to guess what they were talking about.

'And did you read the *Gazette*?' the vicar continued, 'there's a reward being offered for The Lost Sun. Again! I don't mind anyone visiting, but I don't want another break-in to the vestry. I've said a thousand times, it's not in there!'

'The Lost Sun?'

'Old religious artefact. Bejewelled, apparently.

Disappeared from the church years ago, nobody really knows when – could be in Timbuktu by now, not under our noses in the treasure cupboard.'

'Treasure! How exciting,' said Luke.

'*Don't* get any ideas! I've seen that metal detector in your hall.' The vicar squeaked her trainers loudly on the stone floor. 'I'm not having geo-phys wafted all over this church. I ask you. Even if they radared the entire place, what would they find? Nothing. There's been nothing found for centuries, not even the crypt!'

'The crypt?'

'Supposed to be hidden under the church.'

Luke looked down at the floor. 'Why hide it? When it's to remember people?'

'Too easy to hide *in* more like. Old Vicar John told me a homeless man lived in the church for months without being found. They thought there was a ghost until he left a thank you note and a box of chocolates. Never found where he hid.'

Luke nodded, moving his hand from side to side wafting an imaginary metal detector over the floor.

'Prayers then?' said the vicar, steadying Luke's arm.

Little Spirit felt suddenly hopeful, he had recognised an English word "treasure", el Tesoro in Spanish, his language. He had learnt a little English with his father from an old pirate storybook but that was it. He desperately wished he could speak English and could talk to them, they might even help him. But he remembered the man who had promised to help them off the ship at the port.

The man who had split up his family.

He was the first to get out of the shipping container. The crack in the door of the iron crate was so narrow he was the only one able to slip through it. He waited and waited on the dock, hiding behind the other containers, waiting for the bad man who never came. The man they had paid to come with the papers, open the door and get everyone out.

From the cold dock, Little Spirit had watched it, the container with his family inside moved onto land. And in the mix of huge, steel boxes that all looked the same he had lost them.

Lost them. He could barely think about it.

He walked into the road leading to the docking area, hoping that nobody would stop him, but a man caught sight of him and he had to run. The man chased and chased, driving Little

Spirit far from the docks, far from the love of his family.

From that moment, Little Spirit decided to stay hidden. He would stick with his plan to work alone.

He watched the vicar and Luke walk down the centre of the church. They stopped and bowed at the altar before disappearing around a wide stone column. Knowing he would need somewhere safer to hide, Little Spirit slithered under row after row of pews, until he too reached the front.

Very slowly, he poked out his head like a tortoise emerging from its shell. His eyes followed the sunlight swooping down from the high, arched windows, and like blankets of kindness, wrapping itself around the shoulders of Luke and the vicar.

Little Spirit knew you could see kindness everywhere if you looked for it – it lived in his mother's eyes and in his father's gentle hands and especially in his baby sister's lopsided smile – and without them, the soothing light was the closest to kindness he had been since he had lost them.

He dragged his eyes away from the morning light and slid back under the bench pausing to think for a moment. They might not pray for long and he must find a hiding place. He looked back along the path through the centre of the church and upwards to a large balcony. Perfect! But where were the stairs?

Holding the curtains under his arm, Little Spirit crept up the side aisle. He ducked behind the back-most pew and looked up and down. Arm sticking out, he was about to crawl across to a door in the wooden panelling, but suddenly he yanked it back.

The inner doors of the church buff-buffed against each other and somebody came in.

Little Spirit held his breath as two large wheels rolled across the stone floor. The wheels, threaded with blue and white ribbons, belonged to a wheelchair which stopped by a noticeboard. After a moment or two and a rustle of paper, they reversed and trundled back out of the church.

Little Spirit sighed with relief and ran towards the door, stopping briefly by a large stone bowl filled with water. He couldn't help himself and gulped down as much water as he could.

Next he opened the heavy wooden door. Peering around it, he saw a narrow staircase leading up to the balcony. He carefully climbed the steps, begging the old stairs not to creak. A few seconds later, he reached the top and crawled under another wooden pew.

Looking down over the church, with the old curtain wrapped around his shoulders, Little Spirit felt like a king watching over his realm. And it was from there that he presided over the comings and goings of the church visitors, waiting for the moment when it was empty and he could slip out to find food.

A while later, several more people arrived for morning prayers. As they left, two ladies appeared with cloths and old vacuum cleaners that made a loud rattling noise. At midday, Little Spirit jumped in fright as the church bell rang, which brought in an old lady, resplendent in lilac. She sat on the back-pew eating sandwiches and sponge cake. There was no way he could creep past her to the doors.

Little Spirit's stomach howled. He hoped she couldn't hear it.

The lady finally scrunched up the paper-wrapping of her sandwiches, put on her coat and, with a bristle of her shoulders, walked out of the church.

Time slipped quickly on and the short winter days meant the sun soon started to fade from the glass windows. Little Spirit didn't want to be outside in the dark again and now shaking with hunger, he decided it was time go.

Listening out for the buff-buff of the main doors, he crept down the staircase. Halfway down, he found a toilet and a few steps further he glanced inside a cleaning cupboard. He looked at the old, cracked sink and then at his dirty hands. His head swirled with thoughts of bananas.

Washing would have to wait.

A few seconds later, wrapped in the old curtain and the soft evening light, Little Spirit slipped out of the church. He crept across the cobbles towards a row of shops where he saw two boxes dumped on the pavement. Opening the flap of the biggest he peered inside. His eyes widened and his heart nearly burst, bananas – his favourite! Looking around, he quickly stuffed a bunch under the old curtain, vowing one day to repay the shop.

Standing inside a neighbouring doorway he devoured three in a row and leant his head back on the wall. It was even better than eating the first grapes of harvest, after months of waiting for them to become juicy and sweet.

People passed by but no one seemed to notice the boy dressed in an old pair of curtains.

No one except a girl wearing red wellingtons whose brown eyes stared out from under her curls.

It took a few moments for Little Spirit to notice her. He lowered his head and eyed her from under his fringe. There was something familiar about her curly cloud of hair, but he didn't want to be noticed and darted back towards the main street.

He glanced down at his filthy jacket, broken sandals and old curtains. Somebody was bound to question him soon; boys wrapped in orange curtains didn't usually wander the streets alone.

Outside a shop with rainbows on the windows he found several plastic bags, the largest hanging open. Inside, Little Spirit found all he needed: t-shirts, jumpers, trousers, a clean coat, socks and even a pair of battered trainers. He grabbed them all – he didn't have anything else, his rucksack was still inside the shipping container.

With a little bow and a word of thanks, again he vowed to repay the shop.

He dashed round a corner and into a small alley where he pulled on the large jacket and blue trousers; he'd take off his old clothes later. Looking a little more like a local boy; the old curtain neatly folded and tucked under his arm, bananas safely in his jacket pocket, he walked quickly back to the church.

Halfway along the narrow cobbled street he stopped, wondering if he should search for the bus stop. He had clothes and food. He looked skyward where the last fingers of light clung to the clouds. What if he couldn't find the bus stop and was locked out of the church? Where would he stay then? He wouldn't last another night in winter's cold hands.

He'd get back on the bus tomorrow, first thing. Then he would have the day to travel back to his family. He nodded to himself and continued on his way.

Footsteps clattered behind him.

'It's the ghost!' whispered a girl's voice.

Little Spirit swung round and once again stood nose to nose with the girl and her head-full of curls.

3

REMEMBERING

'So you are real!' she said reaching out a hand to him. 'I thought. I thought you were someone I know. Knew...' She dropped her hand. 'Why were you out last night, alone in the fog?'

Little Spirit looked at her blankly.

'Hurry up, Eliza! It's nearly dark,' called a sharp voice.

The girl whipped round. 'Coming, mum! Just talking to the ghost.'

As soon as her back was turned Little Spirit sprinted away. If the girl's mother saw him, she was bound to ask where his parents were. He dipped down a side road and jumped behind a large dustbin, catching his breath and wondering if she would follow him. He listened and listened and waited and waited, but nobody came, no jumble of curls peeping around the corner.

He swallowed hard and forced a smile. Deep down in his tummy he had hoped she might run after him, maybe help him. But she was a child too, probably the same age. How could *she* help?

It was dark now and covered by the shadows, he slunk back to the church.

Once inside, he climbed the balcony stairs and went into the dark cleaning cupboard. First, he took off his coat and new clothes, laying them carefully on the floor. Then he peeled off his filthy shirt and shorts. He washed in the cracked basin, barely able to take his hands away from the soothing warm water of the running tap. Once clean, he gulped water out of his cupped hands until his belly wobbled.

He pulled on all his new clothes, including the jacket, and then threw the curtains around his shoulders. He hung the damp shirt and shorts behind the brooms and brushes, shut the door and went back into the church, returning to the pile of cushions in the corner. He was gathering them up, dreaming of his next banana, when the doors banged.

Footsteps clacked and the cold November wind blew in.

Instantly, Little Spirit dropped to the floor in the middle of the cushions and flung the curtain over him. He shivered, those footsteps again! The ones he thought had followed him to the church.

The footsteps clicked and clacked. Round

the church they clattered, first one way and then back the other. Up and down, down and up.

Little Spirit didn't dare move.

And when they stopped next to him, he didn't dare breathe. The toe tapped right next to his ear; this was a very impatient, angry foot.

The footsteps finally moved away, the clacks fading like a clock being packed into a box. The back doors buff-buffed and the church grew silent again. Little Spirit let out a huge sigh, but his heart still pounded. Who did those noisy shoes belong to? And why were they following him?

He stayed hidden in his orange bundle, not daring to move. He would wait for the doors to be locked so no one could get in. Luckily, he didn't have to wait very long.

A few minutes later, after hearing the turn

of the key in the lock, he quickly took the curtains and cushions up to the balcony where he felt safest.

He made himself a nest under the back pews and ate a banana. He ate another banana just for luck, and with a stomach soaring up to the heavenly rafters, he quickly fell asleep.

*

Next morning, Little Spirit woke at first light. The warm sun streaked through the balcony windows and tickled his face like his mother did when he wouldn't wake up. Today was the day, he thought. He would find the bus stop, get back on, and get back to his family. Yet although he was glad to be in a safe place with a coat for the winter and food nearby, he crossed his arms and gave himself a hug, he'd never, ever felt so alone.

The vicar and the curate soon arrived and

whilst they prayed, Little Spirit slipped out of the church. He recognised the grave stones he had jumped over two nights ago and retraced his steps, hurrying along the side of the church and down the steps at the back. He turned by the wall that he had looked over and seen the girl.

The street seemed to go on forever, but with a tummy full of bananas he kept walking. He paused by a canal and stood for a moment staring at the totem pole. He'd never seen anything like it! As wide and tall as a tree trunk, but instead of branches and leaves, red faces and painted eagles filled the sky. He hurried through the short tunnel, covering his ears at the sound of the train thundering above him. The Lords of the Earth were not happy today. In Guatemala, they owned the land and trees and did not like trains crashing through their kingdom.

Little Spirit walked out through the tunnel and crossed the road. And that's when he saw it, his friend the bus thundering along. He waved and ran towards the bus stop. Luckily, an older boy was already waiting and the bus stopped. Little Spirit ran as fast as he could, the other boy was already inside. He waved again and reached the bus just as the doors were closing.

'Watch yeeself!' yelled the driver, slamming his hand on the button to re-open the doors.

Little Spirit clambered up the steps. The driver looked at him through his oversized spectacles.

'Got your pass?' he snapped.

Little Spirit looked at him blankly.

'Cat got your tongue boy? Money or your pass I said. Or I can't be taking you.'

He looked at the floor.

'Money,' said the driver, rattling some change.

'El moneda,' whispered Little Spirit, understanding what the man had said. He looked up and shrugged, his pockets were empty.

'Off!' said the driver, waving his hand at the door. 'Off me bus!'

Little Spirit stepped off and the bus roared away. 'El moneda,' he whispered to himself again. How could he have been so stupid! Of course he would need money. In his desperation to get back to his family, he had completely forgotten about it. But he didn't have a single quetzal, or English penny, his father had explained that different money was used in England.

He needed money for the bus to take him back to the docks. But how was he going to get some? He wasn't going to steal, that was certain. He felt around in the pockets of his borrowed coat. One of his fingers got stuck in a hole. The other found his last banana. He had nothing. No treasures to sell.

Treasure! The vicar had mentioned "treasure" yesterday. Was there a hidden treasure to be found? The church would be a perfect place to hide one. With hope blooming in his heart, he hurried back to start looking for it.

Over the next few days, Little Spirit made his home up in the balcony and searched the entire building for treasure. He tapped on stones, riffled through cupboards, and even got into the vestry where the vicar kept her robes. But he'd had to hide at the back of the robing cupboard when she rushed in, grabbed a battered box of chocolates and dashed out. Little Spirit followed quickly after her, fearing if she returned, she might find him or worse lock him in with the robes.

Later that night, he examined all the organ pipes and then crawled under every pew, collecting a few pennies along the way. He wondered how many more he would need for the bus ride? But the coins jingled and jangled uncomfortably in his pocket and the next morning he posted them in the donation box at the back of the church. They didn't belong to him.

Not knowing where to search next, Little Spirit hid in the balcony and watched the church again. Maybe someone else was searching for it too.

And someone else was.

It was his footsteps Little Spirit recognised

first; the angry click and clack on the stone floor.

Hidden deep in the bundle of curtains, Little Spirit peered out through a gap in the material and watched the man, the first time he had seen the black pointed shoes shining beneath his dark suit.

The man whipped through the church not bothering to remove his grey fedora and Little Spirit's teeth chattered as he watched the man's elongated shadow, hands stretched like a bony skeleton, prodding the wall next to the vestry door.

When he had finished, the man spent several minutes staring at the balcony. Little Spirit pressed himself to the floor praying the man wouldn't come up the stairs.

Over the next few days, Little Spirit began to feel this man's presence before he saw him: a sharp rush of wind and a distant click told the boy he was approaching. Without seeing him he knew the man was there, just like the great Earth Lord his family prayed to when they built their house by the mountain.

The rain had flown down for days and days after they dug the first trench of the new farmhouse. But when Little Spirit's mother explained their need of the land and why they would dig holes and churn his soil, asking him not to send rain or fog until they were done, the rain dried. And through grey clouds The Earth Lord watched them as they borrowed his land and, stone by stone, brick by brick, tenderly created their home. But this human Earth Lord was different.

Sunday of the same week, he visited early. Hidden behind the tallest organ pipe, Little Spirit watched him pray in the Lady Chapel. Prayers finished, the man tried to open the door to the bell tower situated next to the vestry door. Little Spirit heard it creak open but instead of going up the tower, the man touched the wall inside the door, pressing and shoving it as if he were hoping to make the large stones move.

After several minutes, the vicar's voice boomed out from the other end of the church and a second later, The Earth Lord swept out of the side doors.

'Manzana podrida!' Little Spirit whispered to himself in Spanish. A bad apple! That's what this Earth Lord reminded him of, all ripe and shiny on one side but brown and bruised on the other. Yet the man had shown him something he hadn't noticed before – the church tower and he hadn't searched in there!

Little Spirit watched the vicar go into the vestry and wondered if he should run straight into the tower, but he decided to wait until she had left and snuck back up to the balcony. Just in time.

TA-DA-DA-DAAAA!

A chord from the organ announced the start of Sunday Service.

As quick as a mouse, Little Spirit wriggled into the curtains. Nobody sat in the balcony for this service and peeking out from under the folds, he watched the choir file in. He lay quietly listening to the words of the vicar, not that he understood very much, but the steadiness of the voices and familiarity of the ceremony made him feel a little more at home.

At the end of the service, he watched solemnly as everyone bowed their heads and followed the vicar out of the church and into a fogless morning.

After checking the church was empty, Little Spirit unwrapped himself from the curtains and looked down through the balcony window where the congregation had gathered around a stone monument, covered in letters. One by one, rings of red flowers were placed around it.

He peered at the faces of people watching and smiled, there was the girl again. But his smile quickly faded. Stood next to a young boy in a wheelchair was The Earth Lord, scarf pulled high up his face, eyes fixed upwards…glaring. Little Spirit stumbled back from the window.

'Remember…remember,' boomed the vicar, her words floating upwards.

Little Spirit closed his eyes and wished the man would go away. And he wished he was home, standing on the plain, with his mother and father and his tiny sister, cutting the grapes and listening to the hush of the morning breeze. He missed the farm; his farm of meadows and vines and sheep, protected by the three great volcanos. But he missed it as it was, before the shouts, the gunshots and the burning.

He wanted so much to see his family again, to hug them and laugh with them. He missed them so much he could barely breathe. He rolled under a pew and curled into a ball, pulling the old curtain around him. Remembering really hurt, but it hurt so much more to forget.

Down below the church doors buff-buffed.

Little Spirit held his breath. He waited, listening for the click-clack of The Earth Lord's shoes.

But instead, a girl's voice called out.

'Hello! Are you up there? I've got jam sandwiches if you're hungry?'

4

A FRIEND

Using only one eye, Little Spirit squinted through a narrow opening in the curtains. He saw a jumble of curls and the girl waving something in her hand. It looked like bread. Little Spirit's stomach cramped at the promise of food. But he wondered why she would think a pair of curtains was hungry?

He roved his eye around. Satisfied there wasn't anyone else in the church, he wriggled out of the curtains and crept down the stairs. At the bottom, he opened the door just wide enough to poke his nose through.

The girl tilted her head to one side. 'I'm Eliza!' She sat on the back-most pew, holding out a sandwich. 'What's your name?'

Little Spirit opened the door another inch.

She smiled. 'I won't hurt or bite you!'

Little Spirit furrowed his brow and wondered what she had said. His stomach was growling again, but could he trust her? Would she tell the adults about him? Another gust of wind blew in. Little Spirit watched her curls lift above her kind, brown eyes.

He stared at her for a moment and then looked quickly from side to side. In two leaps he darted across and whipped the sandwich out of her outstretched hand. He dashed back to the door. 'Gracias,' he whispered under his breath. 'Gracias.'

'No need to thank me,' she huffed, not hearing what he had said. 'Are you living here or visiting?'

Little Spirit stared at her, chewing hungrily on the sweet jam and soft bread.

'Perhaps you can't talk?'

A stronger, colder gust of wind blew in. *The Earth Lord*, thought Little Spirit. In a flash, he shut the door, flew up the stairs and disappeared into the bundle of curtains.

The click-clack of footsteps sounded, but quickly stopped. 'Seen a boy?' said a low voice.

Little Spirit froze. Boy. He knew the word "boy" in English.

'No,' he heard Eliza reply. 'No boy here.'

In the tumble of curtains, Little Spirit smiled.

Footsteps click-clacked out of the church.

'He's gone. You can come back down,' Eliza called.

'Down,' whispered Little Spirit. After a

moment, he rolled out of the curtains. He wondered why she had lied and not told the man he was in the balcony.

'You look so like my…' she said, when once more, Little Spirit peered round the door.

He looked at her quizzically.

'Oh nothing.'

Little Spirit watched Eliza sigh as she stood up, and brushed a tear from her cheek. He wanted to comfort her, this kind girl who had brought him food and protected him from The Earth Lord.

Very slowly, Little Spirit moved out from the doorway. 'Pequeño Espíritu,' he whispered, pointing to his chest.

Eliza froze. 'Well, hello Little Spirit!' she said, her face beaming. 'Now, you should know that I know just about everything. And you said your name in Spanish. Español!'

Little Spirit beamed. 'Español!' he repeated, hardly able to believe it.

'Si! I speak pequeño Español! My mum is Spanish.'

'Madre Español?'

'Si! But what are you doing here?' she asked in Spanish. 'Where is your home?'

'Home? It was then that it hit him, right in the stomach, shoving the air up and out of his lungs. It was something he had known the very day he left Guatemala. He knew what he had become. 'I,' he said, 'refugee.'

'Refugee?' Eliza repeated in Spanish.

'A kind of alien. Not from space,' he said, staring at her. 'But from a country a thousand miles from here. It was too scary for my family to live there anymore. I will go back one day. I love my country, Guatemala. But I'm waiting for my family. I'm staying with my aunt,' he lied, inspecting the stone floor.

'Well you look like you're staying here.'

'Just hanging out, I'm looking for treasure.' He added waving his hands excitedly, hoping to divert Eliza from any further discussion about his "aunt".

'Treasure?'

'Yes, the vicar said–'

Eliza shook her head. 'Not The Lost Sun?'

'What's that?'

She turned towards the doors. 'Follow me!'

Bundled up in their winter coats, Eliza and Little Spirit walked out of the church and along the cobblestones. They crossed the main high street and walked up a side road, flanked with tall, brick buildings.

Neither of them noticed the click-clack of shoes pacing steadily behind them.

'Here we are,' said Eliza. 'The library.'

'The what?'

'A place where you can borrow books and look at newspapers.'

'Borrow books?'

'Yes,' she said, with a nod. She walked towards the front window. 'It's closed today but we don't need to go inside.'

Little Spirit stood next to her and peered through the window. The library had walls the colour of clouds and shelves that looked like grey trees growing out of the green carpet.

'Here,' said Eliza, tugging his arm. 'Look at this.'

In the window, hung a copy of a

newspaper, *The Gazette*, and printed on the front was a faded photo of the statue of a sun.

'The Lost Sun,' said Eliza, her eyes growing wide. 'Look at the rubies, it's really, really valuable. There's a reward for whoever finds it and gives it back to the church.'

Little Spirit jumped. 'Reward!'

'Yes, lots of money. But people have been searching for it for years and no one's found it.'

'Well, I'm going to find it,' he said determinedly. 'I need the reward to find my…to get my family here quicker. I haven't searched the tower yet, but the door is open sometimes. That's where I'm going to look next.'

'But it's been searched, again and again.'

'Even the tower?' His shoulders sunk a little.

'Si!'

'Well, I'll search harder,' he said, forcing a smile but feeling suddenly empty. He turned away from Eliza. 'Better get back to my aunt's,' he mumbled, he didn't like lying to his friend.

'Yes, I'd better get home too.'

Together, they walked back towards the church. Little Spirit waved goodbye to Eliza at her house and when her front door had closed, he ducked down behind the wall and crept back towards his home, darting over the grave stones and round to the front door. He stood by the corner of the old Court House adjacent to the church and peered down the cobbled street.

'Oh no!' He ducked down. A few metres away, stood The Earth Lord. The boy in the wheelchair trundled ahead of him.

Little Spirit tip-toed back round the corner. There were only a few steps between him and the church doors, but what if The Earth Lord saw him?

He lay down on the floor, wriggled to the end of the wall and peered round the corner again.

The Earth Lord had turned around and was facing the other way. Little Spirit decided to take a chance. He flew across the path and into the church. He leapt up the balcony stairs two at a time, grabbed the curtains and hauled them over him.

Puffing and panting, he waited, listening for a rush of wind and click-clack of black shoes.

Footsteps sounded, but they belonged to someone else. He lifted a corner of the curtains and peeked out. The curate was scurrying down the aisle towards the vestry carrying a long, metal stick.

THRUM! THRUM!

What's that? It wasn't a sound Little Spirit had heard inside the church before. He wriggled under the curtain, as curious as a cat.

5

TREASURE HUNTERS

The thrumming noise sounded again. Desperate to find out what it was, Little Spirit darted out of the curtain. He jumped back down the stairs and peeked through the door.

The main church was empty and the sound had stopped. Little Spirit hurried down the side aisle and slipped behind the organ, certain the noise was coming from the Lady Chapel. He held on to the smallest pipe and slowly leaned out.

The tower door hung wide open. His foot inched forward desperate to go and search it.

But where was Luke?

Convinced he was in the vestry, Little Spirit

lifted his foot off the step, about to dash across. But he stopped. The thrum, sounding like a giant bee, started throbbing again. It got louder and louder until Luke walked out of the vestry, sweeping the long stick in front of him. It had a plate stuck on the bottom and was making the sound. He wafted the stick up and over the door and went into the tower.

BLEEP!

Little Spirit nearly toppled over. He grabbed the organ pipe.

Bleep! Bleep!

He leant forward to see that the stick had buzzed inside the tower door in exactly the same place where The Earth Lord had tapped the wall. He could see Luke examining the wall too, but he simply tut-tutted, shook the stick and started to walk up the spiral staircase.

Little Spirit wondered what the stick was and why it bleeped by the wall? He took a few deep breaths to calm himself but he couldn't help hopping from one foot to the other. He so wanted to search the tower, convinced The Lost Sun was hidden there. But the spiral staircase was narrow and if he went up, there was nowhere to hide if Luke came down.

Reluctantly he waited, the church was quiet after the morning's service and he could stay hidden behind the organ. He hoped Luke might dash out and leave the door open. Eventually, the curate did hurry out but he locked the door with a frustrated snap. The noisy, metal stick was nowhere to be seen and Little Spirit was no closer to finding The Lost Sun.

*

Over the next weeks, getting into the tower

proved impossible and hiding in the church became very difficult. More people came and went than usual, forcing Little Spirit to stay in the balcony nearly all the time. But here at least, he could watch the arrival of Christmas.

First, a great tree was erected. It was then covered in shiny, glass balls, topped off with a large, golden star. Long banners decorated with trumpeting angels were hoisted high and unfurled down the nave and the smell of fresh fir from the flower-stands filled the air. But best of all was the choir. They practiced almost daily, and to Little Spirit, their voices sounded more beautiful than birdsong.

On the odd occasion he could get out, he tried to stock up on food, but there was much less around; little fruit was left outside shops, and so he had to make do with the half-eaten cakes and sandwiches left on the tables outside the cafes. He hoped to see Eliza again, and always looked out for her bouncing curls.

Worryingly, The Earth Lord now visited every day. Little Spirit's heart twisted into a knot whenever he heard the click-clack of his black, pointed shoes. Sometimes the man stayed in the church the whole morning, moving from place to place on the pews, frequently checking his watch and scribbling notes in a leather book. No one else who came into the church behaved like this, most people had a job to do or came to look at the great windows or to just sit quietly.

No one else would threaten a lost, lonely boy.

It was then that it happened, just after the congregation had walked into the first snowflakes of winter. Little Spirit had taken his position at the corner of the balcony, curtain wrapped around his shoulders like a guardsman's cape.

It was as he lay down to peer through the gaps in the bars of the balcony, that a huge fist suddenly appeared in front of his face.

Thick fingers grabbed the collars of his coat and Little Spirit felt himself being wrenched upwards, whilst another hand was clamped over his mouth. He tried to wriggle free, but The Earth Lord gripped him harder.

Without a word he bundled the boy down the stairs, through the lines of pews, stopping by the door to the bell tower. He dropped Little Spirit on the stone steps, still holding him by his collars.

'I want you,' said the man slowly, 'to get *me* the key to this door, I'll be back in a week.'

Little Spirit looked at him blankly.

'Key,' said the man pointing to the lock. 'Seven days.' He traced the number on the wall with his finger.

Little Spirit shook his head.

'If you don't get the key, I will tell the police you are here,' he said, gritting his teeth. 'T-e-l-l. You. H-e-r-e.'

Little Spirit nodded, he knew a threat when it came, he had seen his father treated like this many times.

The Earth Lord then picked him up, bundled him back to the balcony and dumped him on a bench. In a moment the man was down the stairs, shoes click-clacking, as he walked calmly out of the church.

Shaking all over, Little Spirit stumbled to the balcony window, and stood staring, tears wet on his cheeks. He'd felt safe in the church but not anymore. Even the boat was better than this. Little Spirit and his family had made their journey in relative safety, stowed away on a container ship. He had befriended the ship's cook and helped him in the kitchen in return for secrecy and a hot meal once a day – which kept him and his family alive and together…until they had docked.

Little Spirit gulped and his brain flew into a dark whirl. He grabbed the curtains holding them tight until his breath slowed and his heart stopped pinching.

After a few deep breaths, he could think clearly again. He had grown to love the church, and had explored every inch of it; he knew every stone, every window, which pipes of the organ were large enough to hide in and where the vicar kept her secret supply of chocolate bars. He had got to know the people who cared for the church and he simply could not steal the key. But he couldn't bear to leave either. Besides, he had absolutely nowhere else to go and he really needed the treasure.

Little Spirit ate a banana and sat up in the balcony for the rest of the day, pondering. His father had taught him this discipline, "think long, action quick."

At six p.m. exactly he snuck down the stairs and hid under a pew, close to the tower. He looked across and as he expected, the door was ajar, still open after even chimes. And the key was in the lock. As he moved nearer he could hear muffled voices from the vestry. He had only a few seconds. In a flash, Little Spirit darted over, closed the tower door, grabbed the key and dived under a pew.

'Goodbye, Vicar,' called Luke from inside the vestry, 'I'll lock up tonight.'

'Great! I must skedaddle – it's the school Christmas Concert.'

Little Spirit watched the white swirl of the vicar's robes as she dashed past, followed swiftly by Luke who rushed straight by the tower door, pausing only to lock the main church door.

Little Spirit waited a few moments, just in case Luke suddenly returned. But only the doves cooed softly as he crept into the tower, closing the door silently behind him.

At last, he could search it.

6

CHRISTMAS SPIRIT

There was not a moment to lose. The church was empty and he had the tower all to himself. First, he examined the wall next to the door. What was so interesting about an ancient stone wall? Little Spirit poked and prodded the large blocks, he shoved and pushed them and ran his fingers carefully over them, but the wall gave him nothing more than a scratch from a rusty nail.

He then walked up the spiral staircase and soon arrived at a room filled with ropes running right up to the great church bells. To one side, an upper gallery could be reached by a set of old wooden stairs. The clock chimed, ringing loudly in his ears and he realised this was the home of the church clock machinery.

On his way out of the room Little Spirit peeked inside a small cupboard. It smelt of old socks but was warm and dry and looked like it hadn't been used for years. He smiled, a new hideout, it was getting very dangerous up on the balcony.

Bounding up the remaining steps he quickly arrived at another room. Three huge bells hung sleepily from the roof where several doves cooed. Little Spirit walked around, trying each creaky floorboard as he went. At the far side, he stepped on a board a little narrower than the others.

'Ouch!' he yelped, as it flipped up and he tripped over. He grabbed the handrail and clung to it, not daring to look down at the distant floor, three stories below. Carefully, he pulled himself up and peered into the hole where the floorboard had been. Was there anything inside?

He put his hand inside and felt around the dusty space. Empty. He peered inside to check, and was about to put the floorboard back down, when he noticed a tiny scrap of paper sticking out the side of the hole. He pinched it between his fingers and a leaf of parchment no bigger than his hand slid out.

Little Spirit placed it on his palm and turned it over. On the reverse, in very faint ink, he could see an outline shaped like a cross. He blinked and stared a little closer. Across the middle there were three rectangles, each with faint dots; one on the first rectangle, two on the second and three on the third. It looked like a puzzle.

Little Spirit tucked the paper into his pocket

and replaced the floorboard. Unless it was stepped on, you would never know it opened.

He carried on up the stairs to the very top of the tower. A rusty metal door creaked open and he walked out onto the roof. The wind whipped through his hair and pulled him round to look down over Eliza's house.

From her roof, a skylight blinked in the soft light and he waved, hoping the room might be hers and she might see him. He longed to show her the tower.

The wind whistled again and he noticed the sun had started to set. It would be Evensong soon and the church would be full of people. Little Spirit closed the door to the roof, walked down the stairs, and headed back to the balcony.

*

Seven days later, Little Spirit lay under the back pew of the balcony. With the old curtain tucked around him, he looked like a pile of old rags. He'd spent the week trying to solve the riddle of the little piece of paper, which he thought was a map and found cross-shapes all over the church, but the rectangles remained a mystery.

Peeking out from between the folds, he could see the church quickly filling; men and women, girls, boys, babies and grandparents took their seats. Filling the stone building to its rafters. Stones. Stones were rectangles!

A rush of wind swished into the church and up to the balcony.

Click-clack. Click-clack.

Little Spirit quickly forgot his idea and tightened the curtains around him. Hard, determined footsteps walked towards him.

The footsteps stopped and the point of a black shoe slid under the curtains and stopped. Right next to his left eye.

Little Spirit held his breath. The organ began to play. The Earth Lord's foot turned around as he faced forwards to sing the first carol. The boy shuffled slightly backwards.

He couldn't bear that rotten, stinking apple standing directly above him. He couldn't wiggle away from him but he could wriggle along the line of the pew. Arching his back like a caterpillar, Little Spirit inched forwards, slowly untwining from the curtains.

Like a butterfly emerging from a chrysalis, he stood up and for the first time joined the congregation to watch the service. He loved Christmas and was not going to let The Earth Lord stop him sharing the excitement.

The Earth Lord glared.

Little Spirit pressed his lips together, determined not to let the man see he how frightened he was. He forced himself to smile and then grinned. He grinned more than he had done for weeks, knowing he had nothing to lose if he was discovered and that protected by the crowd of people in the church, he still might escape the man. He may have said 'seven days' but there was nothing The Earth Lord could do.

Or so he thought.

And there he sat, heart jumping and bumping as the church burst with the joy and the love of Christmas. He watched the children as they chattered and carried wooden animals and people to a crib, stood in front of the altar. Luke and the vicar wore golden robes and for just a few minutes, Little Spirit forgot his all worries.

All too quickly, the service ended and Little Spirit watched the heads of the congregation bob out of the church. He looked towards the balcony staircase and then at the man, who slowly stood up.

'Merry Christmas, Sir!' called Luke's friendly voice.

The man swivelled around and Little Spirit shot back under the pew.

'Sorry to rush you,' Luke said smiling, 'we've got another service starting in ten minutes.'

Little Spirit listened to Luke's footsteps and the black shoes click-clack down the stairs. Still wrapped in the curtains, he rolled to the edge of the balcony and peered through the bars. He watched The Earth Lord walk towards the back of the church doors. Once he was out of sight he wriggled out of the curtains. As quiet as a ghost, he slipped down the stairs and through the church. Now for part two of his plan.

Shoes clicked.

The boy stopped, glanced round and saw The Earth Lord striding towards him. 'Quick,' whispered Little Spirit to himself. 'Run!' He dashed into the Lady Chapel, opened the door to the tower and stood in the doorway.

A flash of black arrived first, and then, an open palm.

'No!' said Little Spirit. 'NO!'

Whirling around, he slammed the door. The door handle rattled, but Little Spirit hung on to it and thrust the key in the lock. While The Earth Lord hammered on the wood and dust flew about, Little Spirit locked the door. He stood panting on the stone steps, praying the door would hold. He fled up the stairs and crouched around the first spiral. The organ trumpeted and the hammering stopped.

'Merry Christmas,' said Little Spirit to himself, and knees quaking with both fear and triumph, he wobbled up the stone stairs to his new hideout.

7

THE LOST SUN

'I do believe,' said Luke, as he hung his robes in the vestry cupboard, 'I do believe, that we have a ghost living with us in the church!'

'The Holy Ghost?' replied the vicar with a highly-raised eyebrow.

'No. Yes. No!' he spluttered. 'A ghost…ghost. Very strange things have been happening. I keep having to refill the water in the font, I'm blessing it almost daily, the old curtains seem to move around by themselves, yesterday I found them in a heap up in the balcony. And I'm sure I saw a light in the tower window last night.'

As Luke walked out of the vestry he hesitated by the door to the tower. He stared at the latch, but no key sat neatly under it. Raising his hand, he pulled at the handle – locked.

THUMP! SCRAPE!

'There!' yelled Luke, jumping round. 'Did you hear that?'

'Hear what?' said the vicar, locking the vestry door and scurrying past.

'The thumping!'

'Didn't hear a thing,' said the vicar with an impatient squitch of her trainers. 'Gloves on, the snow's thick outside, and hurry, we'll be late to meet the churchwardens for New Year's luncheon. There'll be plenty of time for Holy…Ghost hunting later,' she muttered, giggling to herself.

While the curate sped after the vicar, on the other side of the tower door Little Spirit stood up. At precisely the moment Luke had turned the handle – Little Spirit had been holding it from the other side. The shock of seeing the door handle turn of its own volition had made him jump sideways so hard, that to his great surprise the stone he had landed on, moved inwards making a loud scraping noise.

And now that Luke and the Vicar had left the church, he pushed the stone again. But it didn't move, not even a tiny bit.

He stared at the stones, tracing his hand over them. A flicker of recognition twinkled in his eyes and his other hand drifted towards his coat pocket, pulling out the small square of paper. The puzzle of rectangles. He held it up in front of the stones. And there it was – a cross.

Exactly like the one on the paper.

Little Spirit ran his fingers over the shape of the cross and the middle three stones. He pressed again and then remembered the little dots. Was it a code? He pressed the stone with the single marking once and the next one along, twice and shoved the final stone as hard as he could three times. On the third shove, to his surprise...whoosh! It slid backwards and moved to the side leaving a hole big enough to crawl through.

Little Spirit dug around the pockets of his oversized coat and pulled out a candle – he'd taken to carrying one – hiding in the tower was very dark on winter days and there were plenty of burnt down candles around the church that wouldn't be missed. He also pulled out a half empty box of matches he found hidden behind the altar.

Candle flickering, he leant forwards and looked into the hole. The light caught on crumbling gravestones, so higgledy-piggledy they looked thrown into the floor, rather than carefully placed. Little Spirit shivered and wrinkled his nose, the rectangular chamber smelt musty and stale. Moving the candle downwards, he saw the floors were thick with dust. No one had been in here recently, despite it being located directly beneath the vestry. He thought of the way he had seen The Earth Lord touch the wall inside the tower door. Was this what he was trying to find?

Little Spirit clambered through the hole and jumped down to the floor. At the far end of the chamber he noticed a wooden door. Circling round the rough stones, he stepped cautiously across to it wondering where it led. A tunnel would be useful, he desperately needed a secret way out of the church; he was running low on food and going in and out of the front doors with

The Earth Lord after him was very frightening.

As he squeezed past the largest head stone, he trod on something soft and mushy. He yelped and quickly bent down. Between two fingers he lifted up a large rag. Shaking the dust off, the faded checks of an old blanket appeared. Was someone else living in the church too? He shook the blanket a little more and dust puffed out like a pair of billows. No, this blanket had not been slept under for a long time.

Little Spirit reached the door and looked up at the thick door panels. There wasn't a lock so, unless it was closed by a latch on the other side, it should open. He steadied himself and with his bony shoulder, shoved the door as hard as he could. It didn't move, maybe it was locked after all. He stood back, determined to get through it. One final heave, and finally, it opened a little.

Holding the candle low, he squeezed through the gap.

'OUCH!' He rubbed his head and swung the candle upwards, eyeing the rocky bumps of the ceiling. As he moved the light downwards, it glinted off the wet, stony walls, walls that seemed to go on and on. Little Spirit quickly forgot his throbbing temple; he was standing in a narrow tunnel.

He walked a few steps forward, lifting the candle up and down, checking the roof height and trying to see how far the tunnel went, but it curved round and he couldn't see any further. He eyed the short candle stub, wondering how long it would last. His tummy rumbled. Desperate to find more food, Little Spirit set off around the corner.

He walked due east for about five minutes,

occasionally batting away thick cobwebs. It was when the tunnel started to slope downwards that he started to pant. The air was definitely thinning. Panicking a little, Little Spirit wondered if he should turn back. But his stomach growled again and he pressed on. On and on went the tunnel until finally, something glinted up ahead.

Little Spirit stopped by a stone wall blocking the tunnel. With only the tiny candle stub as his guide, he tried to breathe slowly whilst he searched for the exit. Looking upwards, he saw rough steps had been cut in a zigzag pattern up and across the wall. He hauled himself onto the first one and, testing each stone as he went, like a mountain goat he climbed steadily upwards.

He only had two steps left when the candle started to hiss. It flickered out as he saw a stone slab directly above him. In complete darkness, his heart nearly thumping out of his chest, he found the last step. Balancing on the tiny ledge, using both hands, he pushed hard upwards.

Bits of dust flew onto his hair, but the stone didn't move. Little Spirit was so desperate to get out of the dark, airless tunnel that he heaved with all the power his thin arms possessed. Finally, the slab loosened and he burst into the winter sunlight among long, frosty blades of grass.

'Where did you come from?' asked a perplexed voice.

Little Spirit froze, looking directly at a pair of red Wellington boots and then at a cloud of brown curls, floating down to investigate.

'Eliza!' he blurted.

'Hello! What are you doing down there?'

Little Spirit looked at her quizzically and climbed out of the hole. He stood up and glanced around a snow-covered graveyard.

'Oh, in Spanish! What are you doing?' she repeated in Spanish.

Little Spirit shook his head and started to move the slab back over the hole. 'What are *you* doing here?' he replied, trying to distract her. He'd be in trouble if anyone found his secret way out of the church.

'Visiting,' she replied, suddenly quiet.

Little Spirit followed Eliza's gaze across the frost-covered stones to a small grave. A posy of dried white roses lay propped against a low headstone.

Together they walked over to the lonely little stone squeezed into a narrow space beside a hedge.

Little Spirit crouched down and read the name. 'Christopherson Jones.'

'My brother,' she whispered.

Little Spirit nodded and gently took her hand.

'When did he die?' He squeezed Eliza's hand even tighter.

'A year ago,' she said, her voice catching in her throat. 'He was very ill, the medicine stopped working.'

'You must miss him very much.'

Eliza nodded. Even her curls didn't have their usual bounce.

They stood for a moment, side by side, hands clasped tightly like the binds of ivy around a tree. At that moment they no longer felt alone in their loss. The wind swirled around them; it whirled and whipped upwards, blowing away over the treetops, lifting their heavy hearts.

And then they could feel the pull of the earth again, feel the certainty of their feet on the ground, their breath in the air, the beauty of the frost on the leaves.

Little Spirit squeezed his friend's hand again and slowly they walked back through the long grass to the tunnel.

'ELIZA!'

They broke hands and Little Spirit jumped back into the tunnel.

'Snails' tails! No need to shout mum!'

'Who were you talking to?' Eliza's mum strode across the graveyard.

'No one.'

'You were definitely talking to something.'

'Just muttering to myself,' Eliza replied, swinging round on the heel of her boot to see if

Little Spirit was still there. But the stone lay flat on the ground and the grass stood as rough and overgrown as ever.

Below ground Little Spirit stood in the dark clinging to the top step.

'Can I walk to grandma's on my own today?' he heard Eliza ask in Spanish.

'Oh! Spanish. Well, ok, but be at the canal in twenty minutes. No later. She'll be upset if you're late for lunch.'

The woman's footsteps faded. Little Spirit heard a knock on the stone.

'She's gone,' Eliza whispered.

Little Spirit pushed his shoulder against the slab and it opened again. 'It's a tunnel,' he said, showing Eliza how to get down the steps. Once at the bottom, and after Little Spirit found a spare candle stub and lit it, they walked back through the tunnel to the church, soon reaching the just-open door to the crypt.

As he held the candle up high to light the way for Eliza, a strange shaft of light blinked through the dark.

'What's that?' said Little Sprit, moving the candle nearer to the new source of light. Again, it blinked from above their heads. On tiptoes, he peered into a shallow hole in the rocky wall. Tucked in a corner, half-wrapped in frayed cloth, something glimmered. He gave the candle to Eliza and heaved the object off the shelf. Very carefully, he pulled down the sacking.

Eliza whistled. Little Spirit's eyes grew as large as planets. They looked at each other and then at a statue moulded in the shape of a golden sun. Little Spirit touched the large rubies and emeralds set at its centre.

'You've done it!' squeaked Eliza in Spanish. 'You've found The Lost Sun!'

Little Spirit's hands started to tremble. He quickly steadied them so he didn't drop the statue. He hardly dared believe it. If he could claim the reward, he could use the money to get on the bus, find his parents and perhaps even pay for a house to stay in.

'Could it be a fake?' said Little Spirit suddenly fearful.

'I don't think so, hard to make a fake look that old,' said Eliza, rubbing the dust off the glittering jewels. 'We should tell the vicar.'

Little Spirit beamed. 'But I'm going to leave it here on the shelf. No one has found it for years. I'll put it back until we need to show it to her.'

Eliza nodded and then looked at her watch.

'Oh no! I'm late! Mum and grandma will be so angry,' she said in rapid English.

Little Spirit looked at her blankly.

'Mum, mad! Not good,' she said in Spanish.

Still hardly able to believe he'd found it, Little Spirit heaved The Lost Sun back into its hidey-hole. They squeezed past the door to the crypt and wriggled back through the hole in the tower wall.

Little Spirit pressed his ear to the tower door. All was silent. He unlocked it and Eliza slipped out.

'I'll tell mum,' she said. 'Tell her about The Lost Sun and…you.'

Little Spirit stopped. 'Non, non!' he cried, as Eliza ran into the church. Nobody must know he was hiding, not until he had claimed the reward. He was going to get back on the bus the second the money touched his hand and he didn't want anyone stopping him.

He leant out of the tower door, shouting for Eliza.

A black pointed shoe tapped on the floor. 'Well, well, well,' said The Earth Lord.

8

THE CHASE

In less than a second, the black shoe flew towards the door. Little Spirit grabbed the handle and tried shut it, but the point of the shoe wedged it open.

Little Spirit leant on it with all his might, gritting his teeth as he battled the man. Slowly, the door began to scrape open. He whipped round, pushing his feet on the steps and forcing his back into the door. But the door creaked and suddenly, Little Spirit went flying, face first, onto the stone stairs.

'Can I help you?' called the distant voice of the curate.

Behind him the door slammed. Little Spirit

peeled himself off the steps, turned quickly and jammed the key in the lock.

'No…thanks.' said the muffled voice of The Earth Lord from the other side of the door. 'Just praying in the chapel. Door was unlocked.'

'Was it?' said Luke. 'I'll have a word with the bell-ringing team, they must have my key. But are you perhaps looking for something?'

'No. No. I'll be off.'

Little Spirit heard the click-clack of shoes as the man started to walk away.

'Lots of people come here to look for The Lost Sun,' Luke called after him. 'Never been found. Not here,' he added firmly.

On the other side of the door, Little Spirit gripped the key tightly, feeling certain they'd mentioned The Lost Sun. What should he do? Turn the key and lock himself in? Or tell Luke that The Lost Sun had been found? Would the curate understand? Little Spirit wished Luke had arrived a few seconds earlier when Eliza was there to translate.

'Goodbye Sir!' called Luke, as the click-clack of The Earth Lord's shoes faded.

Little Spirit stood for a moment shivering and pressing his ear against the door. Where was Luke? What if he heard him turn the key? The lock was old and rusty. Footsteps sounded again. Luke was coming. Then a loud whirr and a crunch echoed through the tower.

Little Spirit looked upwards. The clock! The clunking grew louder and while the machinery noisily churned another hour to its close, Little Spirit locked the door. Not a second too late!

The handle dipped suddenly and the door

rattled. 'Odd!' said Luke from the other side. 'The man said it was open.'

Little Spirit sighed a huge breath of relief but waited by the door until he could no longer hear Luke bustling around. He eventually sat down on the bottom step wondering what should he do now? When would Eliza come back? He even wondered if he'd really found The Lost Sun? Had he simply imagined it all?

Pushing the stones again, he wriggled back into the crypt and into the tunnel, returning to the shelf where The Lost Sun was hidden.

Staring at its golden rays, his heart again burst with hope, reminding him of the early morning light from the great windows at the back of the church. He didn't understand why, but when he sat in the bright, hopeful sunlight it seemed to bring his parents and tiny sister close to him, and he knew somehow that they weren't far away, perhaps just around the corner.

Little Spirit ran his fingers along the sharp groves of the sunbeams. Should he tell Luke or the vicar right now, without Eliza? He worried they wouldn't understand Spanish and might think he had stolen it. He really needed Eliza, she was the only person who could help him. But how could he find her?

Once again, Little Spirit heaved The Lost Sun back into its hiding place and walked out of the tunnel back into the crypt. He wriggled through the hole and started to panic when he got stuck halfway. He shook his leg but it wouldn't move; his trouser was caught on something.

Eventually, he managed to shake it off and climb out. He reached back through the hole, searching for the thing his trouser leg had caught on. He found an iron leaver which felt rough and lumpy against his hand. He thought of the red-hot fire that would have forged the heavy iron rods. A warm fire. That was it! He had seen a fire in Eliza's house on the first night he arrived. Smiling to himself, he pulled the lever and closed the tunnel. Of course he knew where to find her!

*

Next morning, Little Spirit walked quickly through the tunnel and climbed the steps into the bright, chilly day. Coat wrapped tightly around him, he weaved his way through the graveyard and stared across the road, knowing exactly which house was Eliza's.

But today there was no fire, no warming light. Little Spirit thought about knocking on the door, but what if Eliza's mother answered it? He waited for what seemed like hours, but no one came in or out of the house, so he decided find some food and return later.

He walked down the road towards the canal and trudged along the towpath; long boats docked there and someone might have left some rubbish behind. The cold wind whipped off the water and caught on his cheeks. His tummy rumbled. He walked into a short tunnel. And when he emerged out of the other side, a huge shadow loomed down. It reminded him of The Earth Lord when he had threatened him on that terrible day. He started to run and bowled straight into a tall log with bright faces painted on it.

'Do you like our totem pole?'

Little Spirit swivelled round.

'Got back just in time!' said Eliza grinning, her curls whirling in the wind.

Little Spirit grinned and his heart nearly

burst, he was so happy to see his friend. 'Hola! Something bad happened,' he blurted in Spanish. 'The Earth Lord was there, after you had gone. Can you look after The Lost Sun for me?'

'Si!' replied Eliza. 'But can't *you* keep it at your aunt's?'

Little Spirit didn't know what to say. He stood and shook his head. 'Not safe,' he muttered.

'Not safe?'

The boy looked at the kind, brown eyes of his friend. He so wanted to tell her everything.

Eliza sighed. 'I told mum. I told her you're a refugee, not a ghost. But mum didn't quite believe me, said I should ask my friend the refugee-ghost some questions. Ask him to tell me everything, and then she might be able to help.'

Little Spirit stared at his friend. If he didn't

trust her, what else would he do? He held out his hand. 'Vamos!' he said, pointing towards the graveyard. 'And I'll tell you everything.'

Eliza took his hand and then they were off, bounding along. Little Spirit told Eliza, in Spanish, all about The Earth Lord and his threat and that he had nearly caught him. He told her about his mother and father and little sister, about the boat and the bus. He felt very ashamed, but he told her he'd lied about having an aunt and that he was hiding in the church.

And all the while, he hoped her mum wouldn't mind her being friends with a lost boy. A lost son.

Moments later, they raced through the graveyard's creaking gates and zigzagged around the headstones, Little Spirit's coat flapping and Eliza's curls jumbling around in the wind. They were running so fast that they didn't see The Earth Lord creeping up the road behind them.

They didn't feel his eyes on their backs as they reached the far corner of the graveyard, heave up the stone and disappear into the ground.

9

THE TOY

Quickly arriving at the other end of the tunnel, Eliza held the candle stub while Little Spirit carried The Lost Sun through the crypt. They had agreed to take it straight to Eliza's house.

'What was that?' said Eliza suddenly. 'Thought I heard something.'

Little Spirit stopped and listened, but the crypt remained eerily silent. 'Let's go!' he said, pulling the lever to open the exit. Eliza waited while Little Spirit heaved The Lost Sun into the tower stairwell.

Footsteps sounded.

'Quick!' yelled Eliza, 'someone's coming!' She shoved Little Spirit forward and scrambled through the hole.

Behind her, The Earth Lord barged in the crypt. 'MINE!' he yelled lurching towards them.

'Close it,' said Eliza shaking.

In a flash, Little Spirit leant inside and yanked the lever that sealed the entrance.

An angry thump sounded from behind the wall.

'You hide and I'll get mum!' said Eliza, flying through the tower door and out of the church.

Little Spirit puffed his way up the winding stone steps and past the door to the ringing chamber. His arms throbbed, feeling like they would come out of their sockets the statue was so heavy, but he must go higher. Up and up he climbed, his muscles blazing. Every now and again he stopped, ears pricked, listening for sounds from below. He desperately wanted to call out to check Eliza had escaped, but she had run like a hare through the graveyard and he was certain she would get back home.

The boy stopped at the bell room, remembering the small trap door he discovered in the wooden floor. With a last surge of strength, he dragged the statue around the back of the bell and laid it in the space under the floorboards.

Footsteps hammered up the stairs. The Earth Lord must have got out of the crypt. The boy ran out of the bell-room and tiptoed up the winding steps to the top of the tower. He reached out to the door leading to the roof, and listened. The footsteps had stopped.

Little Spirit guessed the man must be searching the ringing chamber. The boy reluctantly opened the door, knowing there was nowhere to hide. He looked to the angle of the sun in the sky hoping the bell-ringers would soon arrive for their weekly practice. He then peered across the sloping zinc roof and looked down at Eliza's house, thinking he might see her hair bobbing along, but several parked cars blocked his view.

The boy moved back to the doorway and listened. Silence. He decided the only place to hide was in the triangular space between the turret-wall and where the door would open. There was just a chance he might not be seen. As he closed the door and took his position, he heard them – footsteps pounding the stairs again.

Moments later, the door burst open. Little Spirit stood trapped between the door and the wall. He sucked in his stomach, as if it would somehow make him invisible. He looked down as the ground seemed to be moving under his feet. Very slowly the point of black shoe appeared.

DONG!

The great bell chimed.

The bell chimed again and Little Spirit waited. Waited for the man to reach behind the door, grab his collars, and haul him roughly down the stairs. He began to shiver, feeling as frightened as it was possible to feel. He ached for his father, begged for him to appear, to stand between him and The Earth Lord.

But as swiftly as it had opened, the door to the tower slammed and Little Spirit was left on the roof with nothing but the lonely north wind.

Shock took over his body and he couldn't move. He stood completely still, watching the shadows grow, waiting until they were stretched long and thin before he had recovered enough to go back inside.

He walked cautiously down the steps, stopping to check under the trap door. He patted The Lost Sun, lying safely in the hole. He made his way down the next flight of steps to the ringing chamber and saw the cupboard door was ajar. His hands started to feel clammy, something wasn't right. He peered inside it and his breath stuck in his throat.

His precious curtains lay torn and ripped, dumped in a heap. He knew instantly the bad apple that had done this. Sinking to his knees, he gently gathered all the pieces, clutching them tightly. Gently and carefully he laid them out, piecing them together, every last scrap.

Satisfied the curtains were back as they should be, he finally left the cupboard. He wasn't angry or sad. He didn't know how he felt. He wondered if feeling nothing was the best way to be. Neither dead nor alive. He walked down the rough stone steps and pressed his ear against the tower door. Gently, he opened it three inches, enough to squeeze through.

Standing inside the chapel, Little Spirit heard a sniff and a cough. He threw himself down, pressing himself close to a step that ran the length of the chapel floor. Silently, he slithered across to the other side and crawled under a pew. The cough sounded again, sounding somehow familiar. Still flat on the floor, he peeped out.

There was The Earth Lord, sitting on a bench with his head bowed, clutching his pocket. He coughed again and from it pulled out a tiny blue bear.

Little Spirit thought the man looked as if all the life had been stolen from him. He couldn't help but feel sorry for him. Little Spirit understood exactly how he felt.

He didn't know how long he lay watching the man, but even after his nemesis had sloped out of the church, he lingered under the pew, wondering. The Earth Lord had frightened him so much, yet clutching a toy, he looked weak and broken to pieces.

Little Spirit sighed. He didn't understand The Earth Lord. He didn't understand the world. He didn't understand why he had been forced to leave his home and lost his family.

He trudged up the tower to the ringing chamber and listened to the clock wind another day to a close. He settled himself in the cupboard, carefully arranging the shreds of the curtains around him, and tried to sleep. He hoped Eliza would bring her mum in the morning.

*

A week later, his sleep still troubled, Little Spirit opened his eyes and quickly closed them again. Dark. How long was the night going to last? Two months had passed since his arrival and he hadn't expected to be hiding under ragged curtains in the musty cupboard of a church for quite so long.

Since the Earth Lord had nearly caught them, he had waited and waited in the graveyard for his friend Eliza. He had staked out her house, but it seemed empty as if she had gone. At dusk, every day, he had walked to the totem pole, thinking he might catch Eliza leaving her grandmother's house. But still there was no flash of red or jumble of curls and it seemed that Eliza had...disappeared.

Worryingly, The Earth Lord had not returned since the day he tried to steal The Lost

Sun. Had *he* locked Eliza away? If the man had captured her, Little Spirit had to find her; it was *all* his fault.

He shivered and pressed his eyes closed. Lately, he had grown to hate the dark of the cupboard and the dark thoughts that it brought him. So that night he sat, not in the tower, but in the church under the great windows wrapped in the last remnants of the old curtain willing the new day would bring Eliza back to him.

But the night had other plans.

10

NIGHT VISITORS

Unable to sleep, Little Spirit left the warmth of his curtains and walked up to the balcony. He looked down through the windows into the shadowy night where a streetlamp painted shimmering orange stripes across the cobblestones. Just like the fire in Eliza's house. He shut his eyes and pressed his nose against the window. If only Eliza would press her nose on the other side like she had all those weeks ago.

Slowly, he opened his eyes again. Something was moving. A shadow stretched across the path and floated towards the church. It stopped for a moment on the front steps, looking furtively up and down the street. Then it dashed towards the church door. Little Spirit flew down the stairs and ran towards the tower. He opened the door and stopped.

No!

It wasn't possible.

The entrance to the crypt was open.

Little Spirit swivelled around as he heard the church doors unlock. Luke's footsteps sounded down the nave. But there was something else. Different footsteps clattered above in the tower.

'The Earth Lord,' said Little Spirit to himself. 'He's got in through the tunnel.' Stood in the tower doorway, he wondered what to do. Stay in the tower? Or risk being caught by Luke?

Without hesitation, he chose Luke. Little Spirit crept back into the church, hid between the tall choir pews and watched the young curate walk down the nave, swinging his torch from side to side. Reaching the front pew, Luke bowed to the altar, turned right and made his way back up the side of the church returning to the font. He peered into the shimmering bowl. 'Water's low again,' he said aloud, shaking his head. His torch wavered nervously in his hand as he shone it up at the balcony.

A few moments later, Little Spirit heard the creak of the stairs as Luke climbed them.

From high up the tower The Earth Lord stomped on the wooden floor. 'Where is that thing? I'm not looking for banana skins!'

Behind the pews, Little Spirit flinched, the shout was muffled and he wondered if Luke had heard it.

From the balcony, Luke shone his torch

down into the church. The light stopped on the font and moved carefully across each row of pews.

Little Spirit pressed himself back into the choir pew and fixed his eyes on the tower door. He imagined The Earth Lord had reached the bell room by now. The floorboard was very loose. Oh, how his eyes would sparkle if he found The Lost Sun and heaved it up from its hiding place. His hand would shake as he pulled it out of its cover to reveal its sparkling jewels.

Distant footsteps sounded. The Earth Lord was coming.

Seconds later, there he was, standing in the tower door, hugging a sack-covered lump to his chest.

Little Spirit couldn't help it. 'Mamá! Papá!' he cried, desperate for help and desperate not to lose the only chance he had of finding his family.

Still on the balcony, Luke swung his torch towards the choir pews. 'Who's there?' he shouted.

The Earth Lord ducked back into the shadows.

Torchlight passed over Little Spirit's head and he peered round the pew. Eyes as wide as the moon, he watched The Earth Lord pull a cap low over his face, turn the collar of his black coat high and sprint through the church.

'I'M CALLING THE POLICE!' bellowed Luke, dashing towards the balcony stairs.

His coat billowing behind him, The Earth Lord disappeared into the night just as Luke burst into the main church. Without hesitating, he raced after him into the dark night.

The church now empty, Little Spirit ran to

the tower door. Maybe The Earth Lord hadn't taken the statue. Maybe he hadn't found it. Little Spirit tried to believe it, tried to convince himself. But standing alone next to the door, he thought he would never find his family.

He stood for longer than he realised and didn't see Luke racing back into the church.

But Luke saw him, a thin, pale vision, shimmering in the chapel.

'The ghost,' said Luke, walking unsteadily towards the main lights. 'The ghost is a boy,' he whispered faintly, clutching at the wall, trying to find the switches.

Snap!

The lights went on.

11

A REUNION

Little Spirit stood rooted to the spot, mesmerised by the bright lights. A thousand thoughts flew through his mind and his throat tightened. He desperately wanted to try, in his limited English, to tell Luke his story, but his head lost the battle to his legs that decided it was time to…disappear.

The boy flew through the tower door and scrambled into the crypt. He yanked the lever and closed the stone hole.

Sounds were muffled from inside the crypt but he could hear the pounding of Luke's steps as he raced up the tower. Little Spirit stood in the dark and waited. A few minutes later, footsteps stomped by again.

Not able to hear anything else, Little Spirit sat in his makeshift bed in a musty corner of the crypt. He had hidden emergency supplies there weeks ago, fearing his discovery in the church. More than ever he desperately needed to find Eliza so he could finally tell Luke his story and claim The Lost Sun. His Sun. Not The Earth Lord's.

She was his only hope.

The young boy spent the next few days hiding behind the wall opposite Eliza's house or in the graveyard waiting for her. Late on the second day, hidden behind the gates, he thought he saw her curls bouncing past but it was a brown-haired boy, jumping puddles.

On the third day, in the crisp February sunshine, Little Spirit lay in the graveyard staring at the grey sky, feeling sadder and more lonely than ever. So much so, that by lunchtime, he had made a decision; if he couldn't find Eliza by the following day, Sunday, he would gather his belongings and walk back to the docks. If he saw someone kind-looking, he might even hitch a ride. A very dangerous plan, but the only one he had.

He worried he might miss his parents if Eliza's mum was helping. They might even be on their way. But how could they be? How could she find them when she didn't even believe he existed? No, they weren't coming to help him. He was definitely going.

The other problem he had was that he couldn't go back into the church. Luke would have found the banana skins and the bits of old curtain and know where he was hiding. The Earth Lord knew about the tunnel and the crypt, so he couldn't stay there. He was completely homeless and he couldn't spend another night in the graveyard.

He slowly opened his eyes to gaze at the sky.

A dark, cloud moved into view. 'Sorry,' it whispered.

Little Spirit sat bolt upright nearly bashing the cloud. 'Eliza!'

'Sorry I didn't come back,' she said in Spanish.

'He didn't take you!'

'Take me! No. Mum grounded me. I was late home after we moved The Lost Sun. She wouldn't believe my story even though I told her everything you said. I make things up a lot.' She lowered her head. 'Get confused.'

The smile that had taken hold of Little

Spirit's face quickly let go.

'But…she believes me now. That man, that Earth Lord. He gave The Lost Sun to the vicar. It's going to be displayed in church tomorrow.'

Little Spirit jumped up.

'Be in church and after Sunday service we'll tell them.' Eliza looked at him. 'And I saw mum looking at an app on her phone called "Ref-something." I think it might help. She's been making lots of phone calls, she said, if I saw you, that you must wait, don't go running away.'

Little Spirit tried to smile, but only managed to set his mouth in a wobbling line. Eliza shook him by the shoulders, 'Be there!' She hugged him tightly. 'Sorry I have to go,' and off she ran.

Little Spirit sat for a moment trying to take it all in. He felt so happy that Eliza was safe, but would they believe his story over The Earth Lord? A lost boy over a grown man? But one thing was certain, whatever happened tomorrow, he was leaving and he needed to say his goodbyes.

At eight o'clock that evening when Luke had locked the church for the night. Little Spirit climbed out of the tunnel, unlocked the tower door and walked into the main church. His fear of The Earth Lord wasn't going to stop him spending his last night there.

All his belongings, including a couple of bananas, were wrapped in a small bag made out of strips of the old curtains. He placed it behind the low-hanging altar cloth so it was hidden from view and went to sit under the large windows.

He then walked a goodbye lap around the church, sitting on the balcony, piling up the prayer cushions, neatening the leaflets and gazing at the pink dove above the altar. He would never forget the church that had sheltered him or the shops that had unknowingly kept him alive.

Earlier that day, he'd left a posy of winter leaves outside the green and white one, which had given him winter clothes. Given him life. He left another posy outside each shop that had left food; they would never know how much he owed them.

Eventually, overcome by fatigue, he lay down behind the altar cloth, resting his head on his bag and hugging the last piece of the old curtains. For the first time in weeks he slept properly.

In fact, he slept so deeply that not even the bright light of the morning woke him, or the chatter of the early-comers. It was only the fanfare of the organ and the bellowing of the churchwarden that finally roused him.

Little Spirit sprang up and banged his head on the underside of the altar. Rubbing his head, he peeked out from under the corner of the cloth and stared straight into Luke's face.

12

AN UNUSUAL FOG RETURNS

Luke dropped the altar cloth. 'Vicar! The ghost is under the altar!'

'Lovely,' muttered the vicar as she broke the bread and blessed it.

Luke looked from The Lost Sun, gleaming on the altar, to the flapping cloth and back, all the way through communion right until the very end of the service.

'And now the banns of marriage,' said the vicar, swinging round to see what Luke was doing.

Behind her, he lifted the cloth again.

Little Spirit gulped and Luke quickly let it drop. Through its heavy swishes, he watched Luke rush into line with the vicar and, followed by the choir, proceed up the nave.

Once the service had finished and the congregation started to leave the church, Little Spirit crawled out from under the altar. Sitting on the cold, marble steps he hugged his makeshift bag. He looked at The Lost Sun, wondering if he should grab it and run, but then he saw Luke. And then he heard them.

A click-clack of shoes.

'He tried to steal it from me!' shouted The Earth Lord, his voice shaking. 'The Lost Sun, he stole it from me'

Little Spirit jumped up.

'Don't let that boy escape! Hold him or he'll run,' shouted The Earth Lord.

Luke swerved around and Little Spirit started to tremble.

A jumble of footsteps ran up. 'He's innocent,' said Eliza in a determined voice. 'His name is Little Spirit and he found The Lost Sun. You stole it from him!'

'Lies!' yelled the man, his face glowing red.

'Let the boy speak for himself,' said Luke.

All eyes turned to Little Spirit.

Eliza stood next to her friend. 'He can't speak English, only Spanish. He's a refugee from Guatemala,' she said. 'He's been hiding in the church and he found The Lost Sun. He showed it to me, but the man wanted it for the reward and stole it.'

'No!' said The Earth Lord, 'it's mine!' He turned, as if about to grab the statue and run out of the church, but something stopped him.

'Dad,' said a frail voice, 'don't lie. I know when you're lying.' A boy in a wheelchair rolled forward and stopped by The Earth Lord. He was no older than Little Spirit, but had a pinched, sunken face.

Little Spirit recognised the boy and his wheelchair. They were the wheels that he'd seen on his very first day at the church.

'Dad didn't mean it,' he said. 'He's trying to help me.'

The Earth Lord hung his head. 'My son is very ill,' he whispered, 'the reward would pay for a special operation.'

Little Spirit listened to Eliza's translation. *The toy*, he thought, *that's why The Earth Lord was holding the blue bear.*

'Goodness me! Mr Farina,' said the vicar, arriving with a squidge of her trainers, 'come everyone, we must sit and discuss what is to be done.'

The vicar, Luke, Little Spirit, Mr Farina and his son, Eliza and her mother sat on chairs by the great window. Holding Little Spirit's hand, and with occasional help from her mother, Eliza told his story.

'Well, The Lost Sun returns,' said the vicar, collecting it from the altar and holding it up to the light.

'What is The Lost Sun?' asked Eliza.

'A Monstrance. It's a statue that we sometimes use in our services, a symbol of our closeness to God.'

'I don't understand,' said Eliza.

'It's like a landmark, or a reminder of how close we are to home.'

'Like the totem pole by grandma's house.'

'Just like that,' the vicar replied, smiling.

'Well,' she added, turning to Little Spirit and handing him the statue, 'there's the reward to settle now.'

A phone bleeped. 'Sorry,' said Eliza's mum, looking worried.

Little Spirit hugged the statue close to him. But while the vicar had been speaking, he had been staring and staring at the boy and Mr Farina. Very slowly, Little Spirit got off his chair and walked over to them.

'You keep,' he said, placing the statue on the seat next to the boy's wheelchair.

The boy looked up. 'Truly?'

Little Spirit nodded.

'Thank you,' said the boy, smiling at Little Spirit and squeezing his father's hand with his thin fingers.

Mr Farina hung his head and sat very still.

'Well,' said Eliza's mum, 'your parents must be mad with worry.'

Little Spirit shook his head and sat down, not able to find the words in Spanish, let alone in English, to say what had happened. He grabbed his bag made of the old curtains and held it close. He had lost his family for ever.

He just wanted to run. To run and run and run until he was too tired to think, too tired to breathe, too tired to feel. He glanced towards the open door and saw it, despite the unusual warmth of the day – the fog had returned.

Little Spirit looked around; Luke and the vicar were in deep discussion and Eliza's mum was talking on her mobile phone; Mr Farina was hugging his son and Eliza was staring at the rubies shimmering at the heart of The Lost Sun.

Nobody would notice. He knew he shouldn't,

that Eliza had asked him not to, but he didn't know what else to do.

And so, he ran.

He flew out of the church and stumbled up the road, dragging himself through the swirls of fog to where he thought a bus shelter stood. Little Spirit heard the distant rumble of an engine. He sprinted on until he saw the grey pole of the shelter.

The mist curled and twined its thick fingers around him. The grumbling engine drew nearer. Little Spirit flung out his hand hoping the driver would see it.

But the bus chugged by, the driver didn't stop for ghosts. In fact, he shouted through the window. 'You ghosts can bloomin' well float to town all by yerselves.'

Little Spirit heard them again, distant

footsteps. He stood on the curb. More engines whined and roared. The fog thickened tugging him towards the road. Pulling him forwards, if he walked forward a little more perhaps a car would stop.

The footsteps were louder now, like an army surging over the top and into battle, shouting and stamping, urging him on.

He stuck out his arm, he could hear the car was close now. Any moment.

The footsteps pelted up to him and just as he was about to step in front of the car, a strong hand yanked him backwards. 'Got you boy,' said Mr Farina. He twisted his hands around the boy's and tugged him back onto the pavement. Very gently, they guided him into the arms of someone else, someone warm and familiar.

It was the hands and arms that he had

dreamt of every night and searched for every day, the hands and arms and love and warmth of a woman, a man and a tiny gurgling girl.

The fog stood still.

Happiness burst out of his fingers as he grabbed his family and they grabbed him. He gripped his father's rough hands and kissed his tiny sister. His mother hugged him so close he knew she would never let him go again. They stood huddled together as tightly as they could, the love of a family burning brighter than the sun, brighter than all the stars in the sky.

And as quickly as it came, the unusual fog disappeared.

Mr Farina looked at the boy and his family. He stepped aside as Eliza and her mother rushed towards them.

'How did you do it?' asked Little Spirit in

Spanish.

'With 'Refunite', the app on mum's phone. Through it she was put in contact with your mum and dad.'

Little Spirit clung to his father. 'Thank you,' he said, smiling at Eliza and her mother.

'Please come with us,' said Eliza, 'mum says so and so do I. You can all stay, we've got space. Until you find your own home, our home is yours. Your home.'

Little Spirit looked at his mother and father, at his sister and then at his friend, Eliza.

He nodded. 'Yes,' he said, '…home.'

THE END

AUTHOR'S NOTE

At the time of publication the UNHCR or the United Nations Refugee Agency reported that, at the end of 2017, there were 68.5 million refugees or displaced people worldwide.

To put this number into context, the current (2018) population of the UK is 66.57 million. So that's more people than our entire country! Imagine all of us in the UK having to pack a very small bag and leave home, not knowing when we would return. We are so fortunate not to be in this situation and live in an amazing and beautiful country, full of opportunity and hope.

There are, in fact, many refugee 'routes' across the world, routes people follow to get to other countries, and they are extremely dangerous. This includes Guatemala and as I developed and researched this story, I read many very sad stories about children who risked everything for a safer, happier life.

There are some cruel things said about refugees in the press and by certain world leaders. But I think it's vital to remember that refugees don't leave their homes without reason. They are desperate. They want to be safe and to live peacefully, that's all.

I hope Little Spirit has given you a small insight into the life of a refugee and, however young you are, if you see someone wrapped in a pair of old curtains, perhaps you too (with the help of your parent or carer) could bring a jam sandwich and the helping hand of friendship.

REFUNITE is a real organisation and you can see the amazing work they do here: www.refunite.org.

ACKNOWLEDGEMENTS

There are so many people I'd like to thank for bringing this book into the world. It's a little miracle really.

I first wrote Little Spirit as a serialised story and got my first publishing credit thanks to Ian Skillicorn, who kindly published my early, not so polished, work. And huge thanks to my early-draft young readers, especially Nell F and Conall T, you were both so enthusiastic that I had to keep working on it.

I'd also like to thank my young advance readers; hearing you are enjoying Little Spirit is the best thing of all.

I wouldn't still be novel writing without the support of my wonderful friend and eagle-eyed writing partner, Megan Thompson. Meg, you are my writing rock and I am so glad we are making this mad writing journey together. And Deb, thank you my dearest, oldest friend, you have patiently read all my early drafts and have given me such great encouragement, insight and support, and importantly, the views of an experienced teacher.

Thanks to Cornerstones for putting me in touch with Jonathan Eyers, your editorial direction helped lift the story to another level, as have all the lessons learned from the brilliant Golden Egg Academy – Imogen, thank you for all you have taught me and for being so incredibly kind. And fellow eggs, it's great being part of the nest with you.

And lastly, my family. Rocco and Cristabel, I love you very, very much. Thank you Rocco for reading my books, you will be able to hold one soon and put it on your bookshelf. Cristabel, I can't wait until you are old enough to read them too. My dear parents, I am so lucky to have the kindest mum and dad, who realised way before I did, that my writing might just have potential.

Finally, thank you Mark, you have never doubted me even though writing and editing books takes forever and ever...and ever! It's a long old road and there's no other hand I'd rather hold along the way.

UNTIL NEXT TIME…

Become an Advance Reader for New Books!
To make sure you get the chance to become an advance reader
of my new books, please ask a parent or carer to sign-up to my
newsletter at my website: **www.whatdomykidsreadnext.com**
– they'll receive very occasional book review round-ups and
news about my latest book releases, and requests to join my
advance reader team.

**In the New Year, I'll be giving away the first three
chapters of my next book – The SuperTech Secrets**, a
space adventure – first in a trilogy, launching March 2019.

You can also catch me on twitter @pjmarvell, or on Instagram,
A J Freer at whatdomykidsreadnext, and on my A J Freer
Facebook page – do pop by and say hello.

If you'd like find out about the amazing writing academy I
belong to, The Golden Egg Academy, you can visit their
website at www.goldeneggacademy.com.

One Last Request – Please Write a REVIEW
Ask your parent or carer to help, and you can leave a review
on Amazon. Just a sentence or two is so helpful. Reviews
really help other readers discover Little Spirit too.

ABOUT THE AUTHOR

Hello, I'm A J Freer or Ange. I've always loved reading stories and as a child was mostly found with my head in a book. I've been learning the craft of storytelling for quite some while now, and found the best place to do this is at The Golden Egg Academy, a writing academy for children's authors.

However, my route to novel writing has been far from conventional involving a university degree in Management Science and French, followed by a Masters in Computing. Working in the City of London was my next stop…and the last, before working out what I really wanted to do – write books for children. All thanks to the amazing JK Rowling.

I live in the UK, in the historic Hertfordshire town where this story is set, with my two children and lovely husband. I can now mostly be found with my head in a laptop, feverishly trying to write my next book.

THANK YOU FOR READING.

ADIÓS!